BY KEAN SOO

STONE ARCH BOOKS
a capstone imprint

March Grand Prix
published by Stone Arch Books,
a Capstone Imprint
1710 Roe Crest Drive
North Mankato, Minnesota 56003
www.capstonepub.com

Cataloging-in-Publication Data is available on
the Library of Congress website.

ISBN: 978-1-4342-9640-5 (library hardcover)
ISBN: 978-1-4342-9643-6 (paperback)
ISBN: 978-1-4965-0185-1 (eBook)

Summary: March Hare's first race for Tuttle
Racing is the infamous Desert Rally. March
and his GT Superturbo must endure extreme
conditions, deadly competitors, and an
unexpected co-driver who has her own agenda!

Printed in China by Nordica.
0415/CA21500596

042015   008843NORDF15

KEAN SOO
MARCH
GRAND PRIX

THE BAKER'S RUN

To Juni,

For providing the first spark.

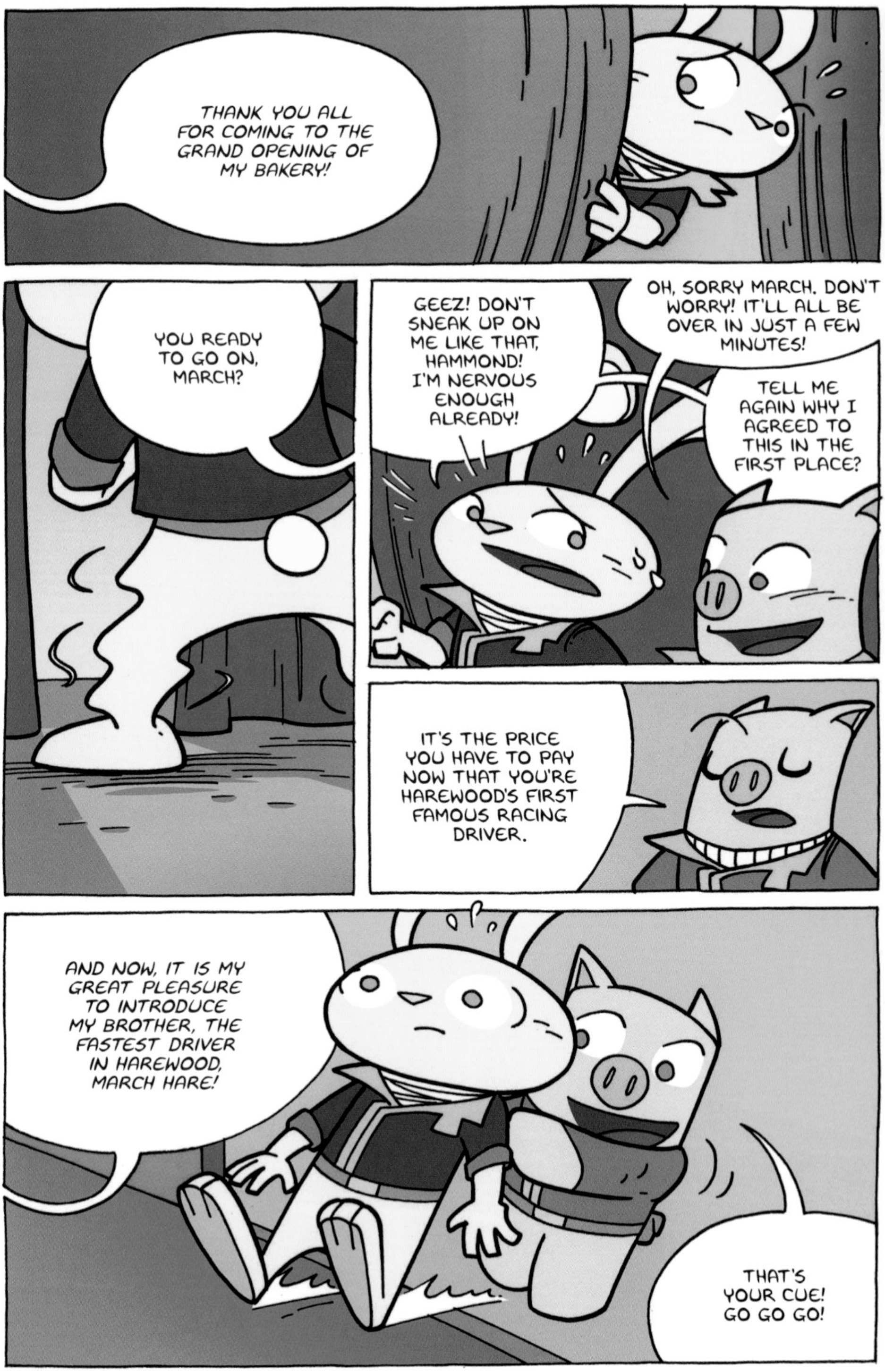
THANK YOU ALL FOR COMING TO THE GRAND OPENING OF MY BAKERY!
YOU READY TO GO ON, MARCH?
GEEZ! DON'T SNEAK UP ON ME LIKE THAT, HAMMOND! I'M NERVOUS ENOUGH ALREADY!
OH, SORRY MARCH. DON'T WORRY! IT'LL ALL BE OVER IN JUST A FEW MINUTES!
TELL ME AGAIN WHY I AGREED TO THIS IN THE FIRST PLACE?
IT'S THE PRICE YOU HAVE TO PAY NOW THAT YOU'RE HAREWOOD'S FIRST FAMOUS RACING DRIVER.
AND NOW, IT IS MY GREAT PLEASURE TO INTRODUCE MY BROTHER, THE FASTEST DRIVER IN HAREWOOD, MARCH HARE!
THAT'S YOUR CUE! GO GO GO!

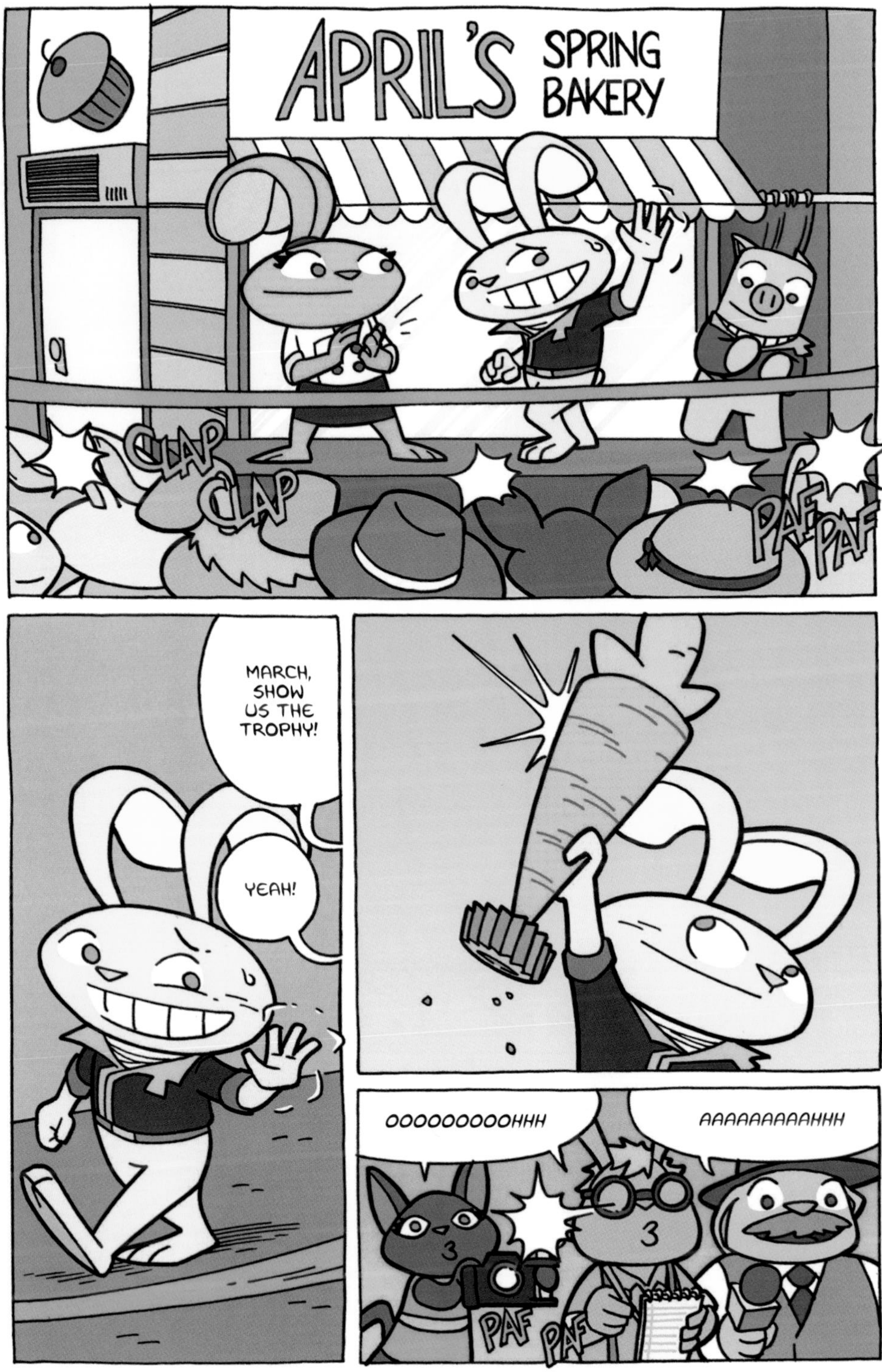
APRIL'S SPRING BAKERY
CLAP CLAP
PAF PAF
MARCH, SHOW US THE TROPHY!
YEAH!
OOOOOOOOOHHH
AAAAAAAAAHHH
PAF PAF

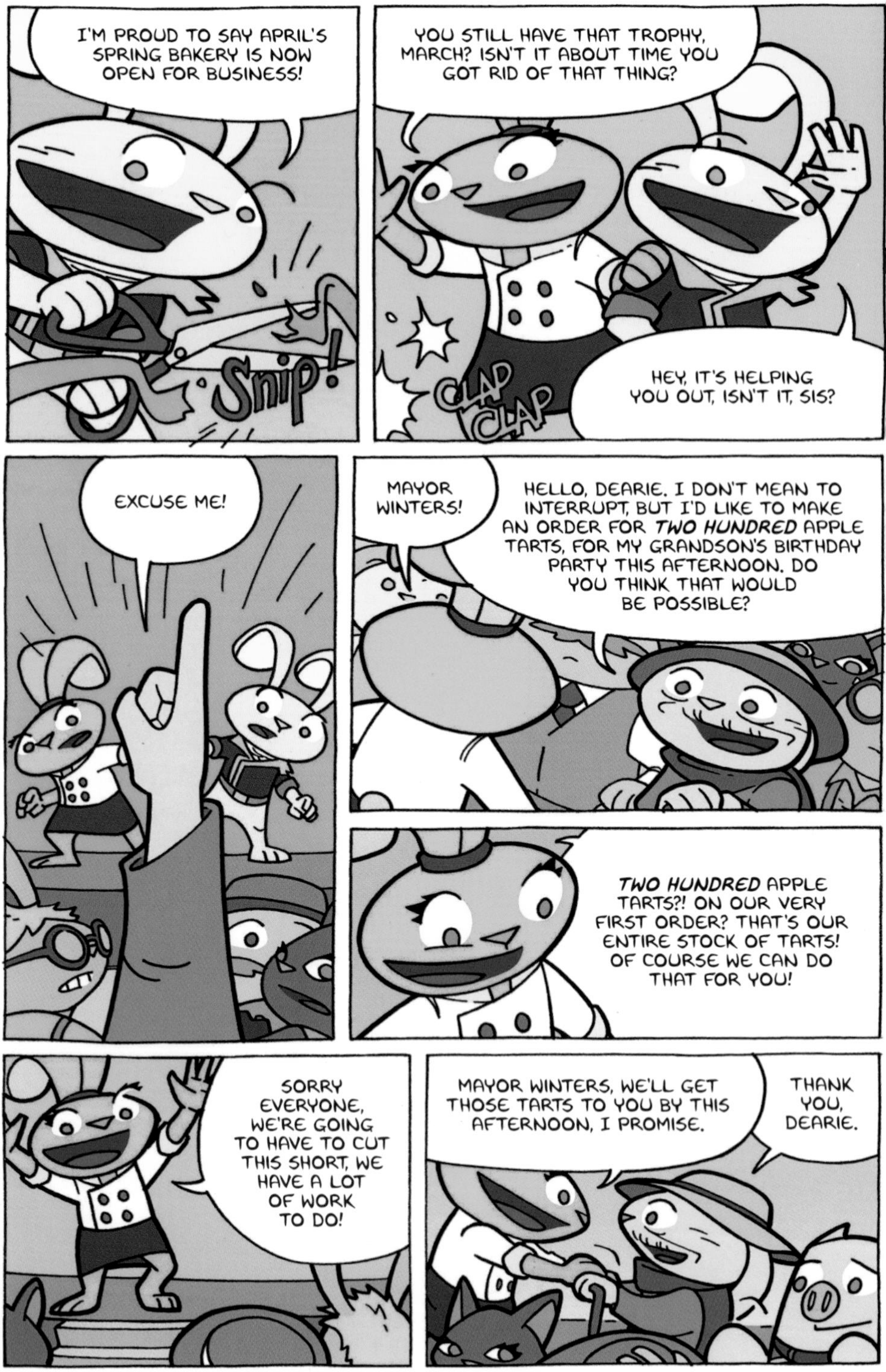
I'M PROUD TO SAY APRIL'S SPRING BAKERY IS NOW OPEN FOR BUSINESS!
SNIP!
YOU STILL HAVE THAT TROPHY, MARCH? ISN'T IT ABOUT TIME YOU GOT RID OF THAT THING?
CLAP CLAP
HEY, IT'S HELPING YOU OUT, ISN'T IT, SIS?
EXCUSE ME!
MAYOR WINTERS!
HELLO, DEARIE. I DON'T MEAN TO INTERRUPT, BUT I'D LIKE TO MAKE AN ORDER FOR *TWO HUNDRED* APPLE TARTS, FOR MY GRANDSON'S BIRTHDAY PARTY THIS AFTERNOON. DO YOU THINK THAT WOULD BE POSSIBLE?
TWO HUNDRED APPLE TARTS?! ON OUR VERY FIRST ORDER? THAT'S OUR ENTIRE STOCK OF TARTS! OF COURSE WE CAN DO THAT FOR YOU!
SORRY EVERYONE, WE'RE GOING TO HAVE TO CUT THIS SHORT, WE HAVE A LOT OF WORK TO DO!
MAYOR WINTERS, WE'LL GET THOSE TARTS TO YOU BY THIS AFTERNOON, I PROMISE.
THANK YOU, DEARIE.

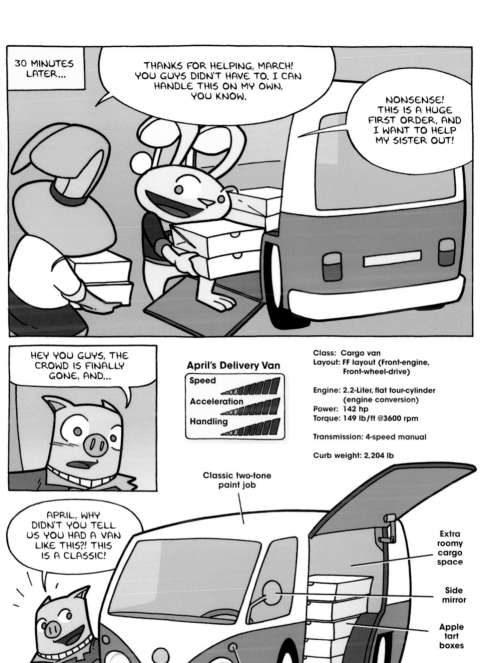

April's Delivery Van

Speed
Acceleration
Handling

Class: Cargo van
Layout: FF layout (Front-engine, Front-wheel-drive)

Engine: 2.2-Liter, flat four-cylinder (engine conversion)
Power: 142 hp
Torque: 149 lb/ft @3600 rpm

Transmission: 4-speed manual

Curb weight: 2,204 lb

Classic two-tone paint job

Extra roomy cargo space

Side mirror

Apple tart boxes

Deep dish wheels

Envious mechanic

Bumper

Headlamp

Turn indicator

Split panel "barn" doors

April's Famous Apple Tart

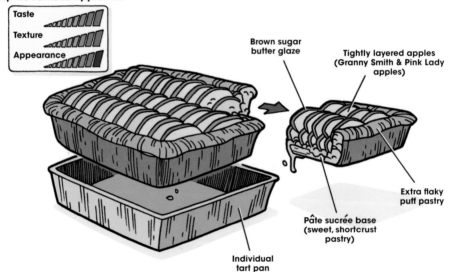

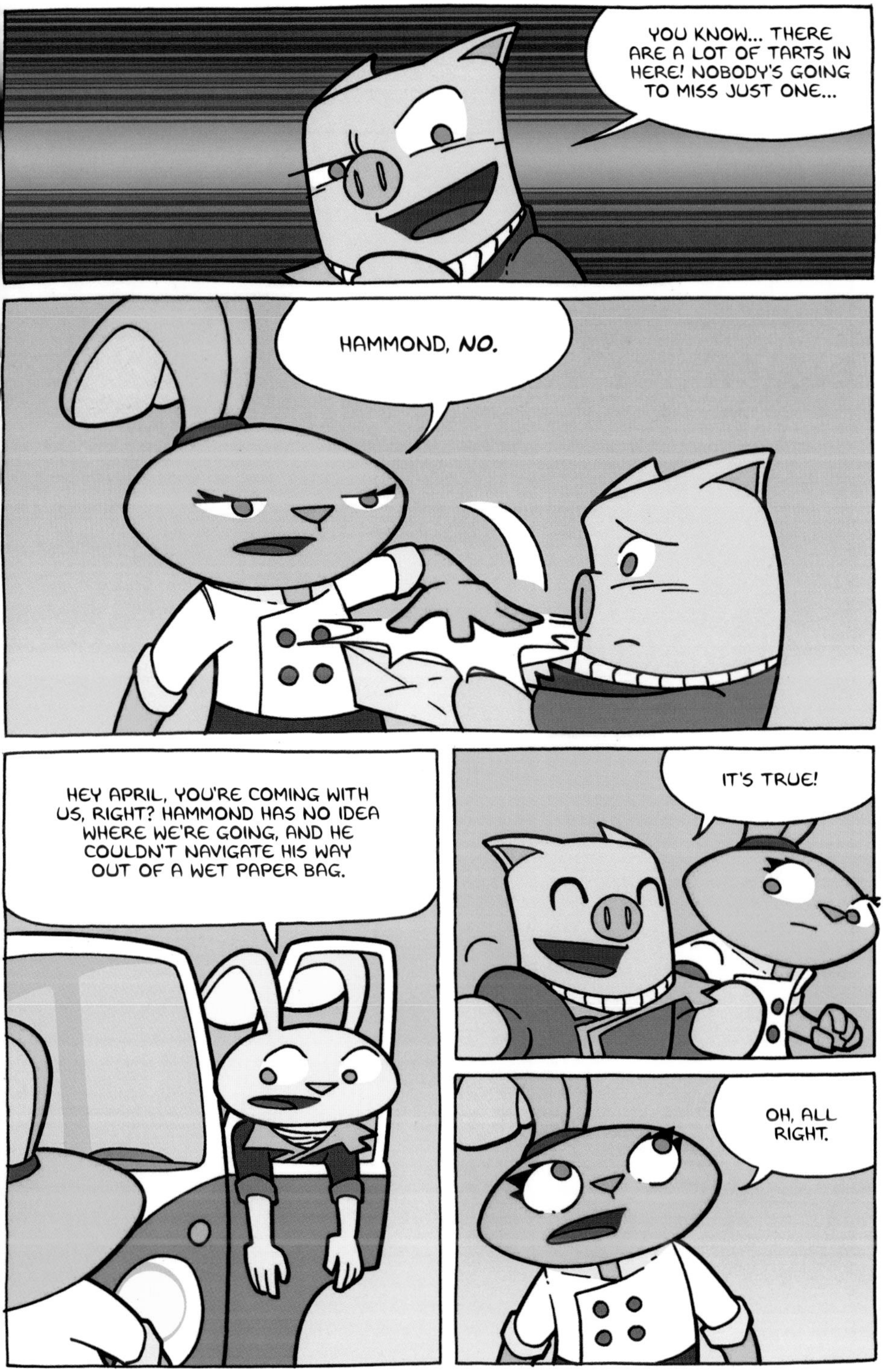
YOU KNOW... THERE ARE A LOT OF TARTS IN HERE! NOBODY'S GOING TO MISS JUST ONE...
HAMMOND, NO.
HEY APRIL, YOU'RE COMING WITH US, RIGHT? HAMMOND HAS NO IDEA WHERE WE'RE GOING, AND HE COULDN'T NAVIGATE HIS WAY OUT OF A WET PAPER BAG.
IT'S TRUE!
OH, ALL RIGHT.

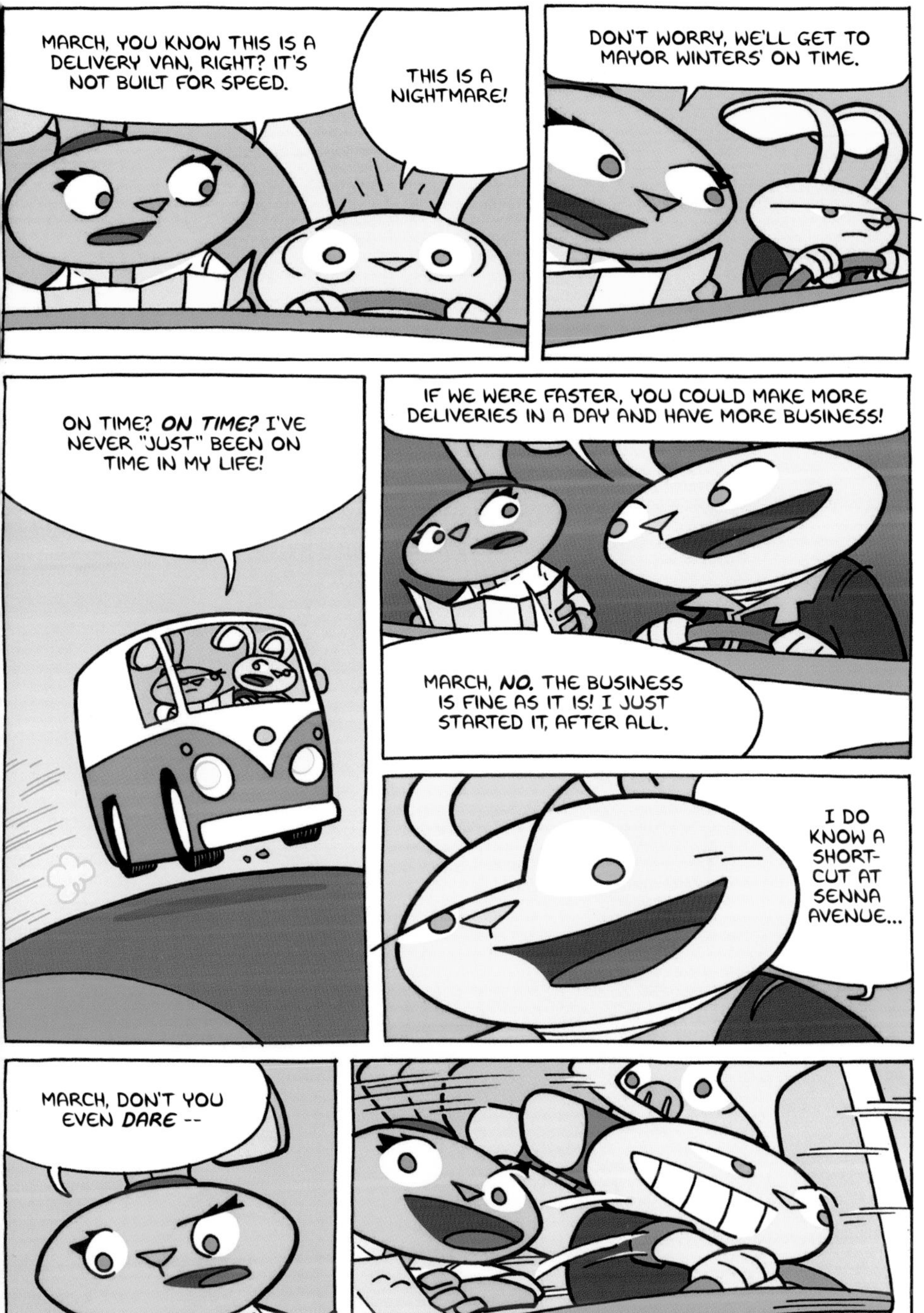
MARCH, YOU KNOW THIS IS A DELIVERY VAN, RIGHT? IT'S NOT BUILT FOR SPEED.
THIS IS A NIGHTMARE!
DON'T WORRY, WE'LL GET TO MAYOR WINTERS' ON TIME.
ON TIME? *ON TIME?* I'VE NEVER "JUST" BEEN ON TIME IN MY LIFE!
IF WE WERE FASTER, YOU COULD MAKE MORE DELIVERIES IN A DAY AND HAVE MORE BUSINESS!
MARCH, **NO.** THE BUSINESS IS FINE AS IT IS! I JUST STARTED IT, AFTER ALL.
I DO KNOW A SHORT-CUT AT SENNA AVENUE...
MARCH, DON'T YOU EVEN *DARE* --
SCREEEEE

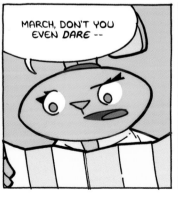

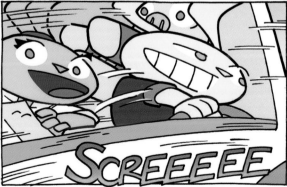

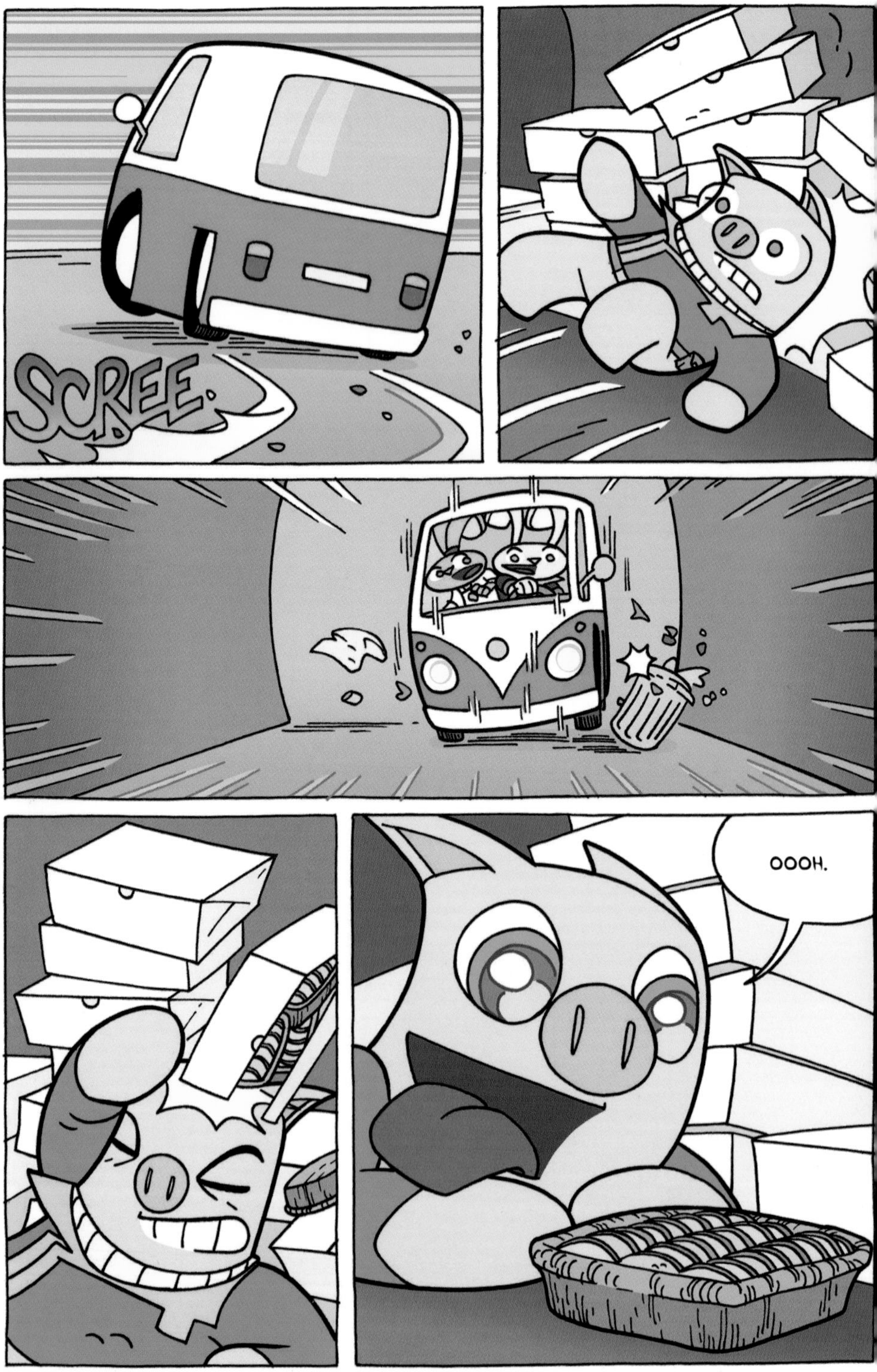
SCREE
OOOH.

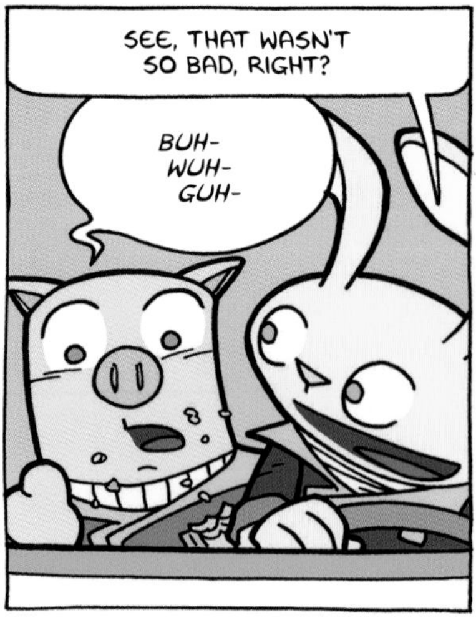
SEE, THAT WASN'T SO BAD, RIGHT?
BUH- WUH- GUH-

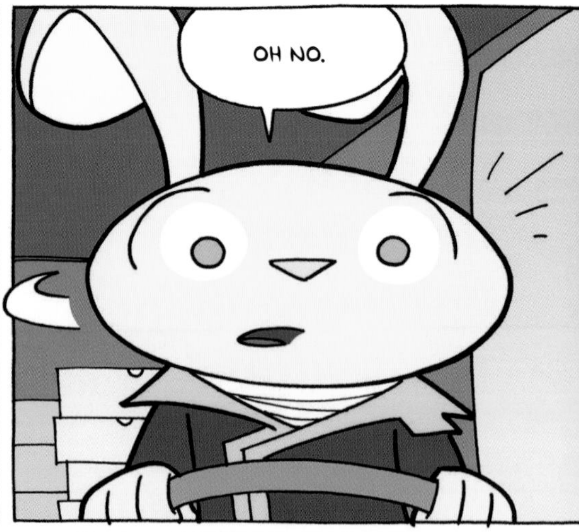
OH NO.

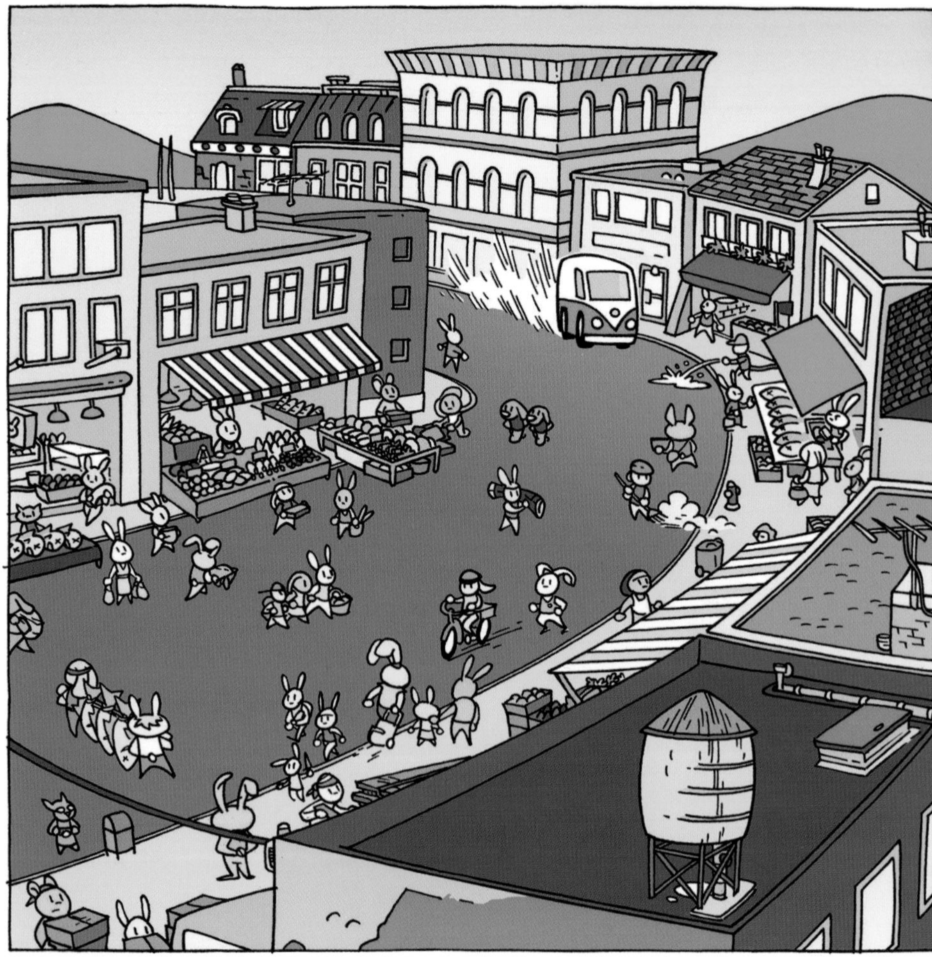

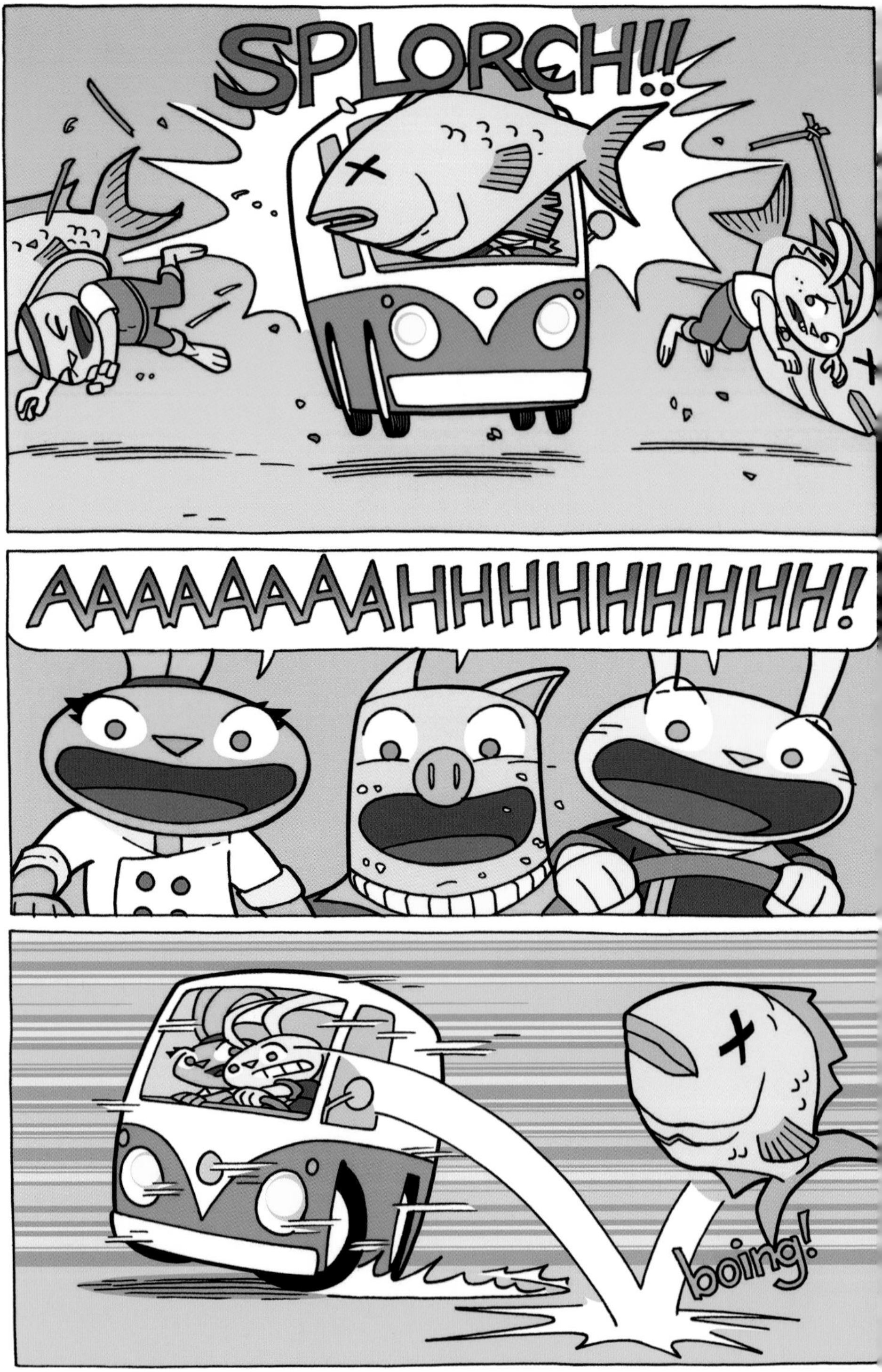
SPLORCH!!
AAAAAAAAHHHHHHHHHH!
boing!

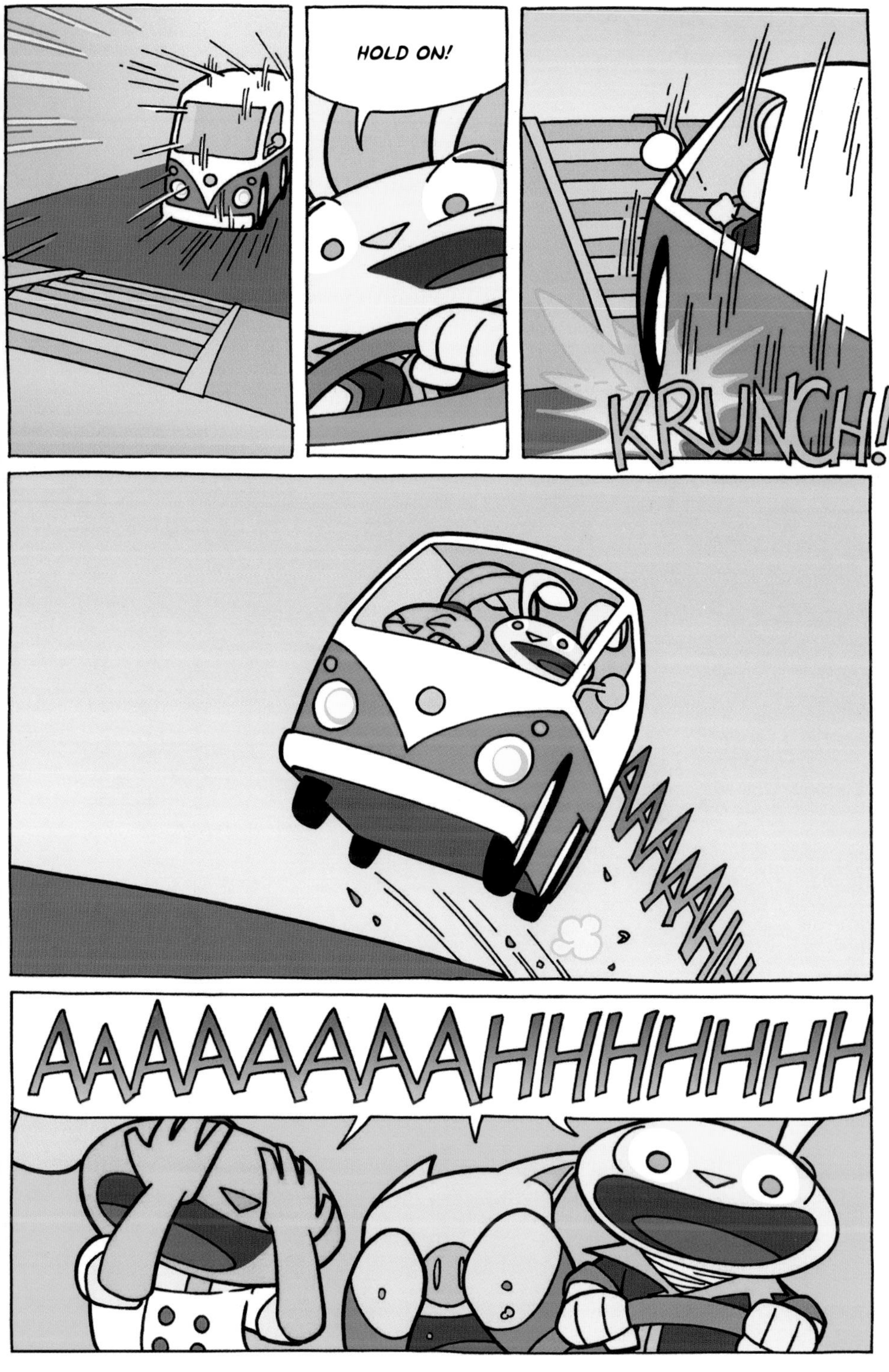
HOLD ON!
KRUNCH!
AAAAAHH
AAAAAAAAHHHHHHH

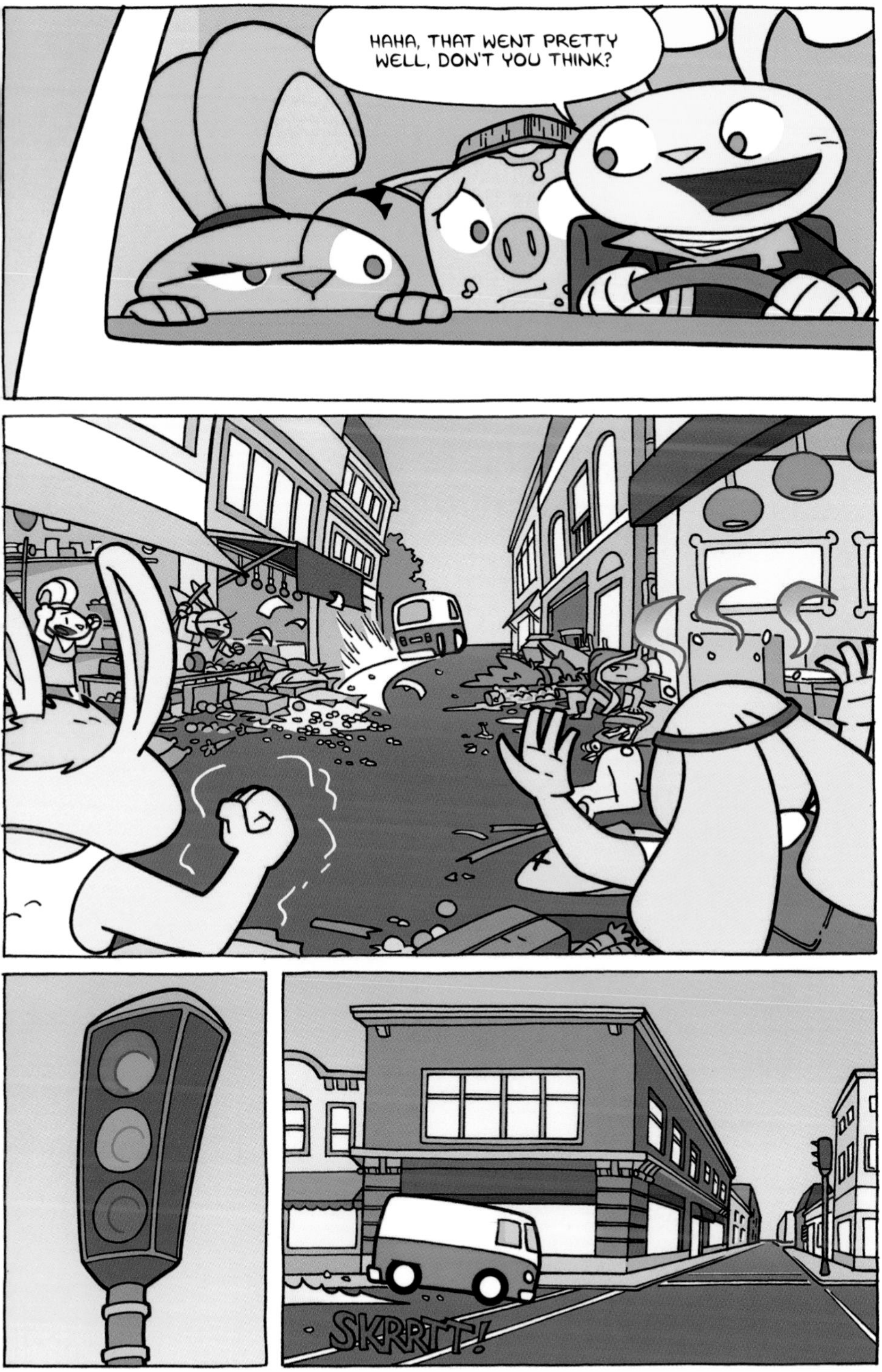
HAHA, THAT WENT PRETTY WELL, DON'T YOU THINK?
SKRRTT!

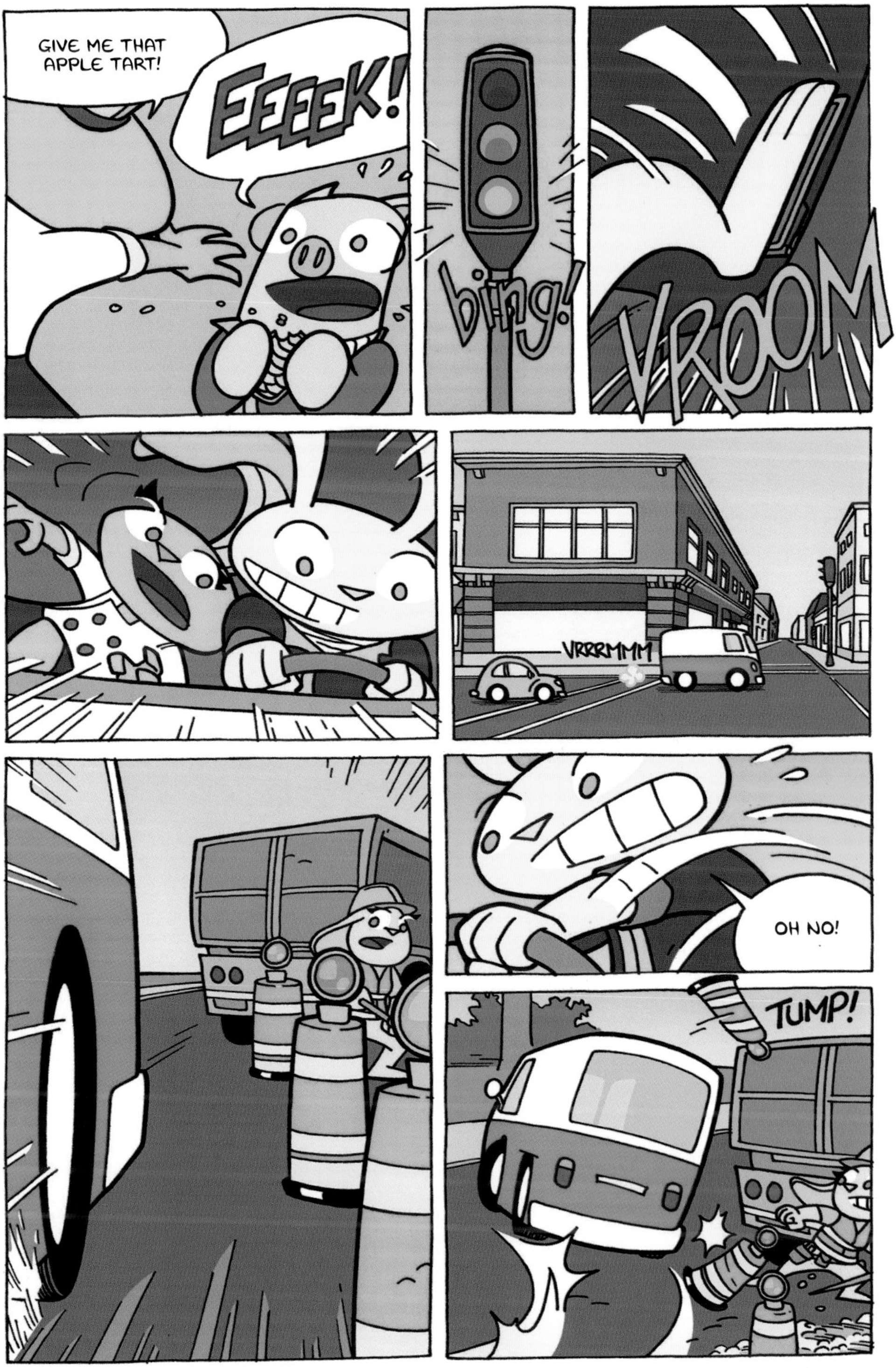
GIVE ME THAT APPLE TART!
EEEEK!
bing!
VROOM
VRRRMMM
OH NO!
TUMP!

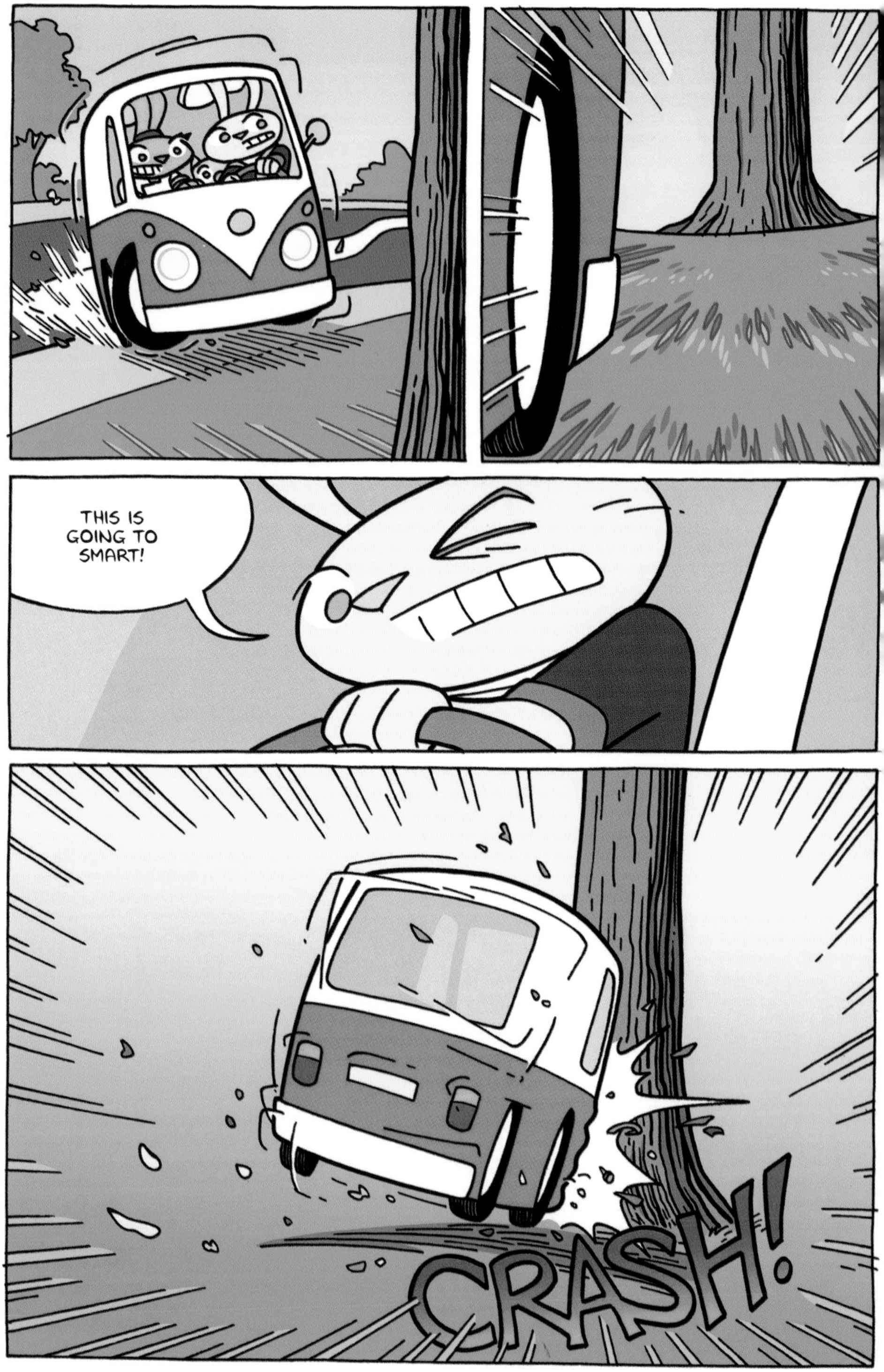
THIS IS GOING TO SMART!
CRASH!

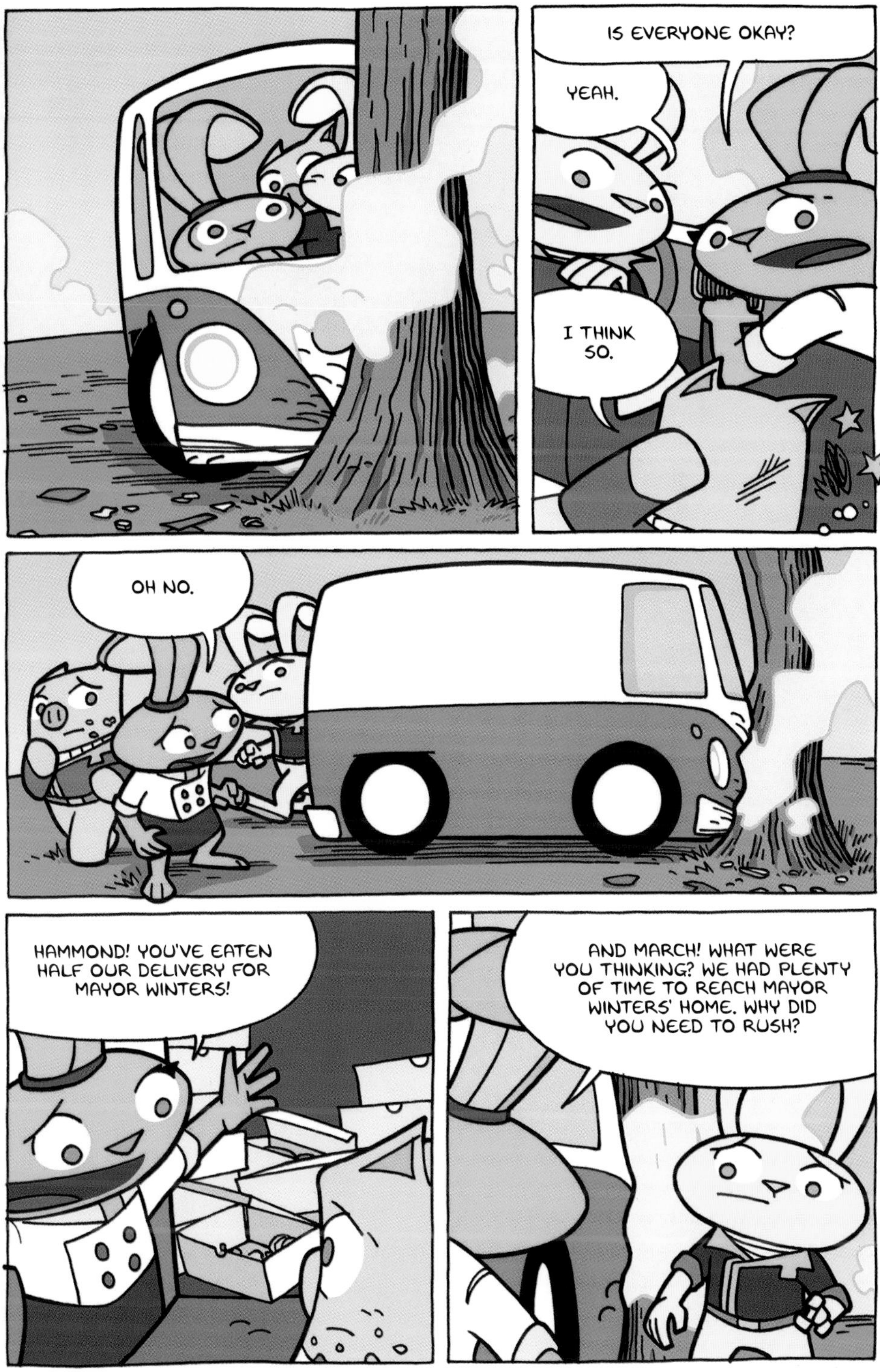
IS EVERYONE OKAY?
YEAH.
I THINK SO.
OH NO.
HAMMOND! YOU'VE EATEN HALF OUR DELIVERY FOR MAYOR WINTERS!
AND MARCH! WHAT WERE YOU THINKING? WE HAD PLENTY OF TIME TO REACH MAYOR WINTERS' HOME. WHY DID YOU NEED TO RUSH?

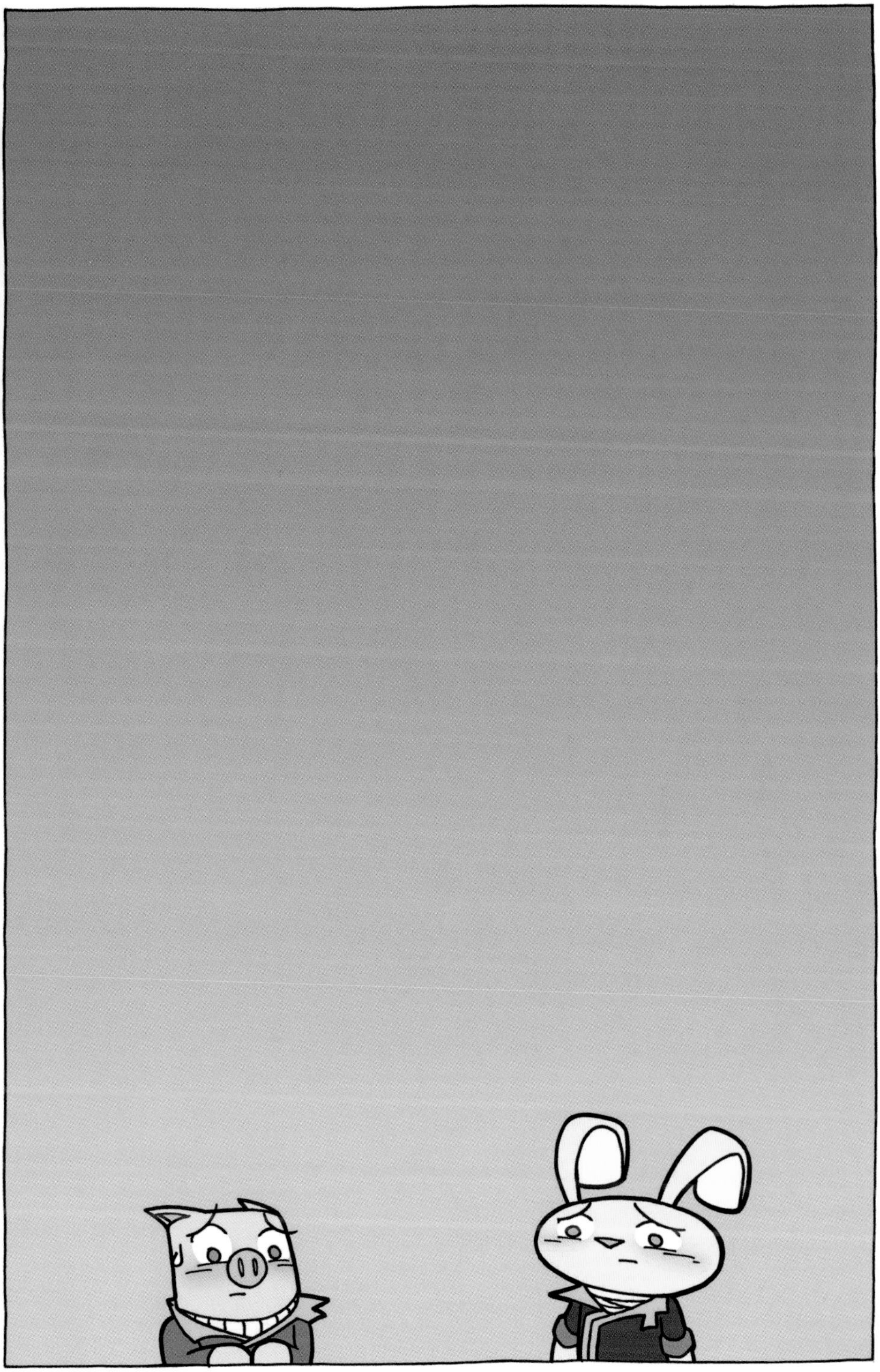

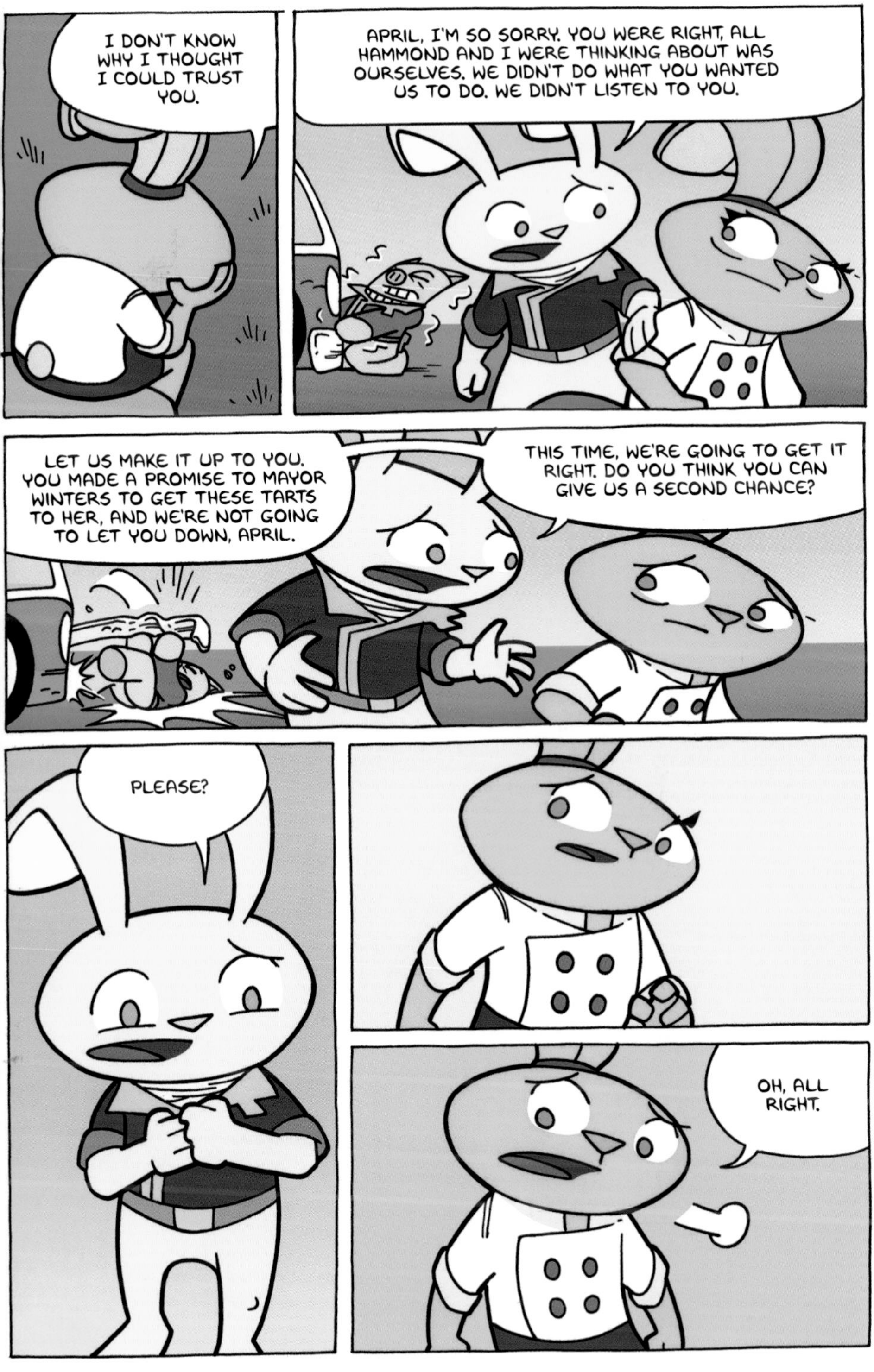
I DON'T KNOW WHY I THOUGHT I COULD TRUST YOU.
APRIL, I'M SO SORRY. YOU WERE RIGHT. ALL HAMMOND AND I WERE THINKING ABOUT WAS OURSELVES. WE DIDN'T DO WHAT YOU WANTED US TO DO. WE DIDN'T LISTEN TO YOU.
LET US MAKE IT UP TO YOU. YOU MADE A PROMISE TO MAYOR WINTERS TO GET THESE TARTS TO HER, AND WE'RE NOT GOING TO LET YOU DOWN, APRIL.
THIS TIME, WE'RE GOING TO GET IT RIGHT. DO YOU THINK YOU CAN GIVE US A SECOND CHANCE?
PLEASE?
OH, ALL RIGHT.

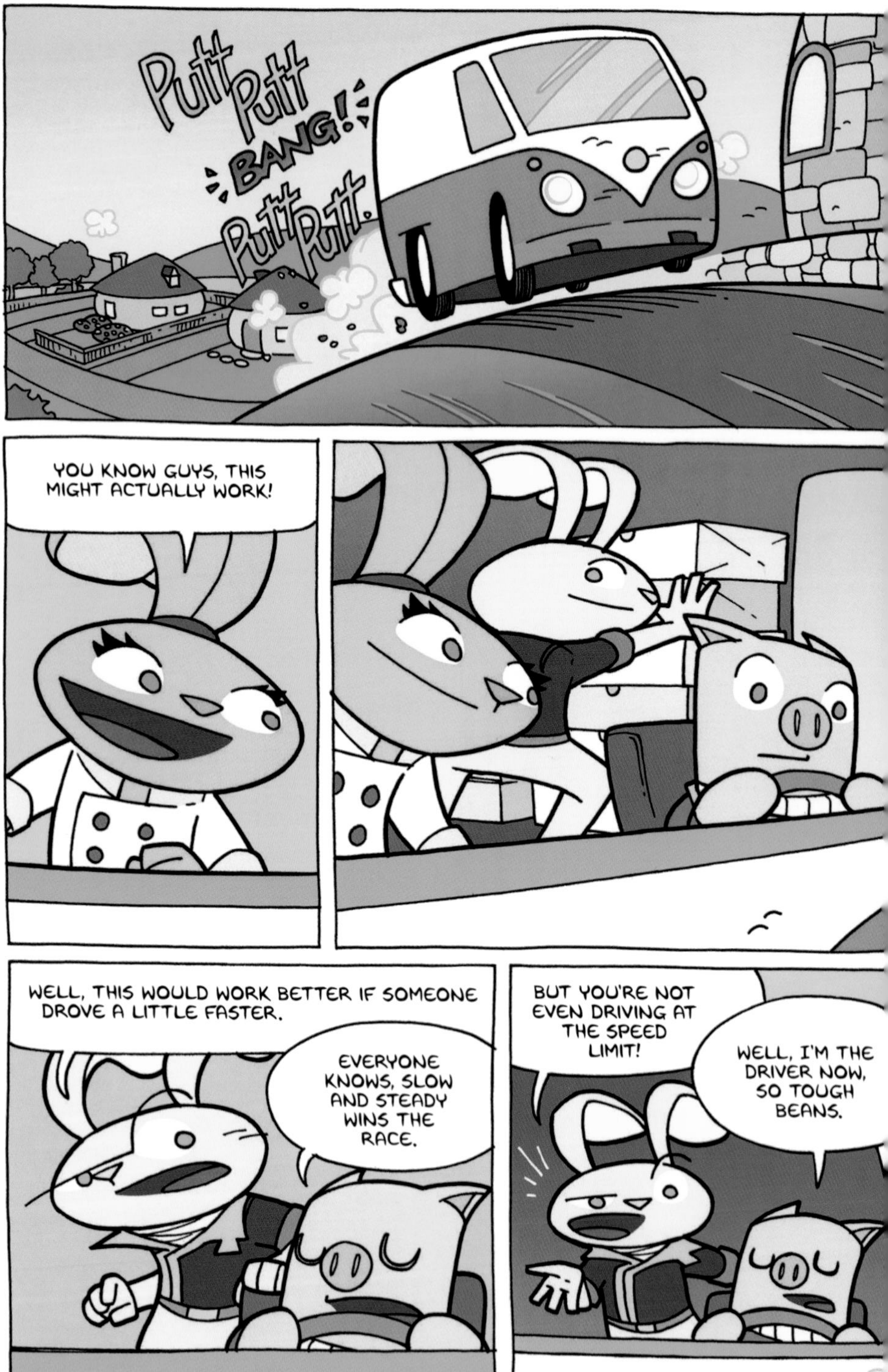
Putt Putt
BANG!
Putt Putt
YOU KNOW GUYS, THIS MIGHT ACTUALLY WORK!
WELL, THIS WOULD WORK BETTER IF SOMEONE DROVE A LITTLE FASTER.
EVERYONE KNOWS, SLOW AND STEADY WINS THE RACE.
BUT YOU'RE NOT EVEN DRIVING AT THE SPEED LIMIT!
WELL, I'M THE DRIVER NOW, SO TOUGH BEANS.

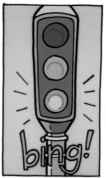

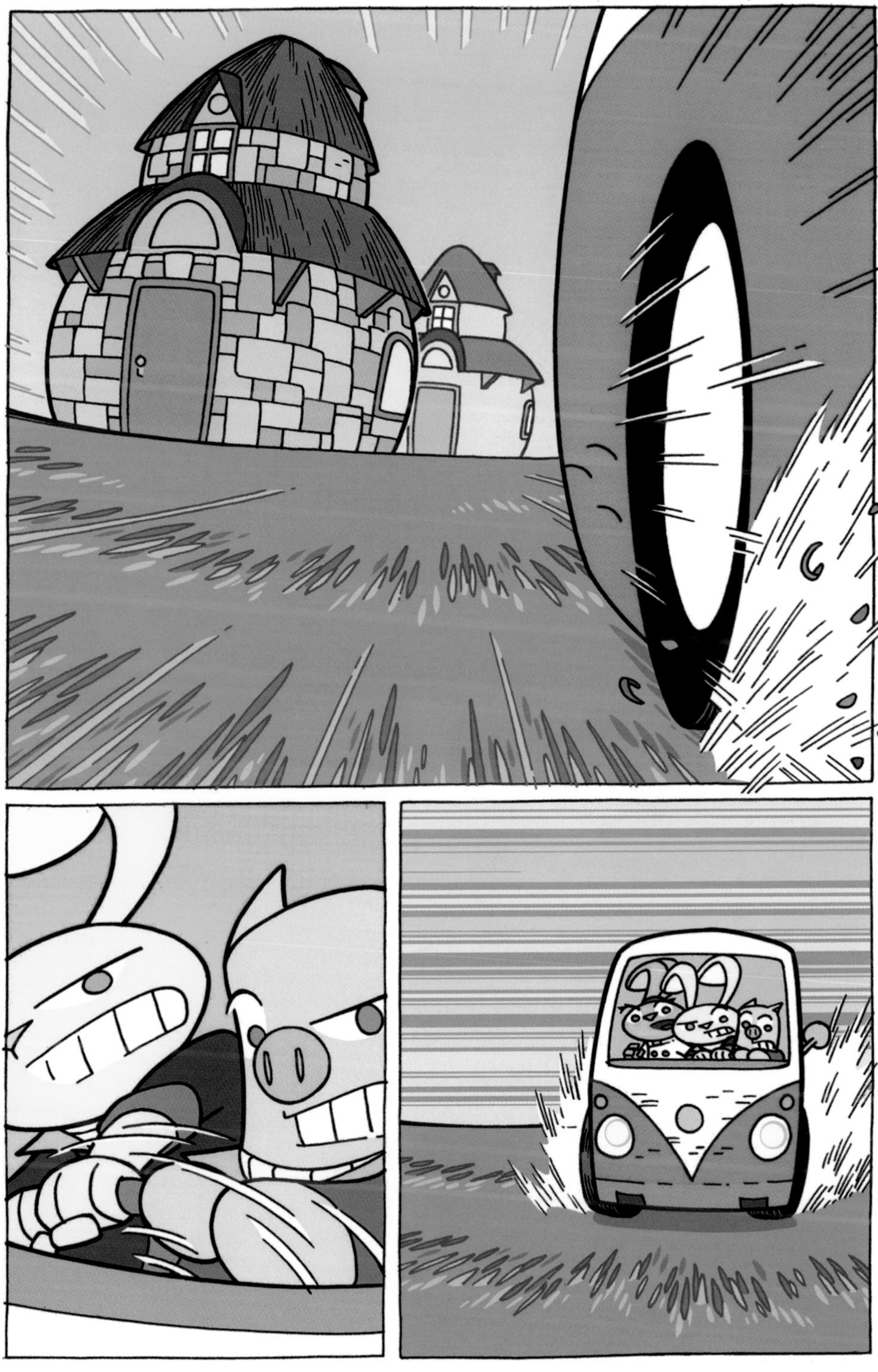

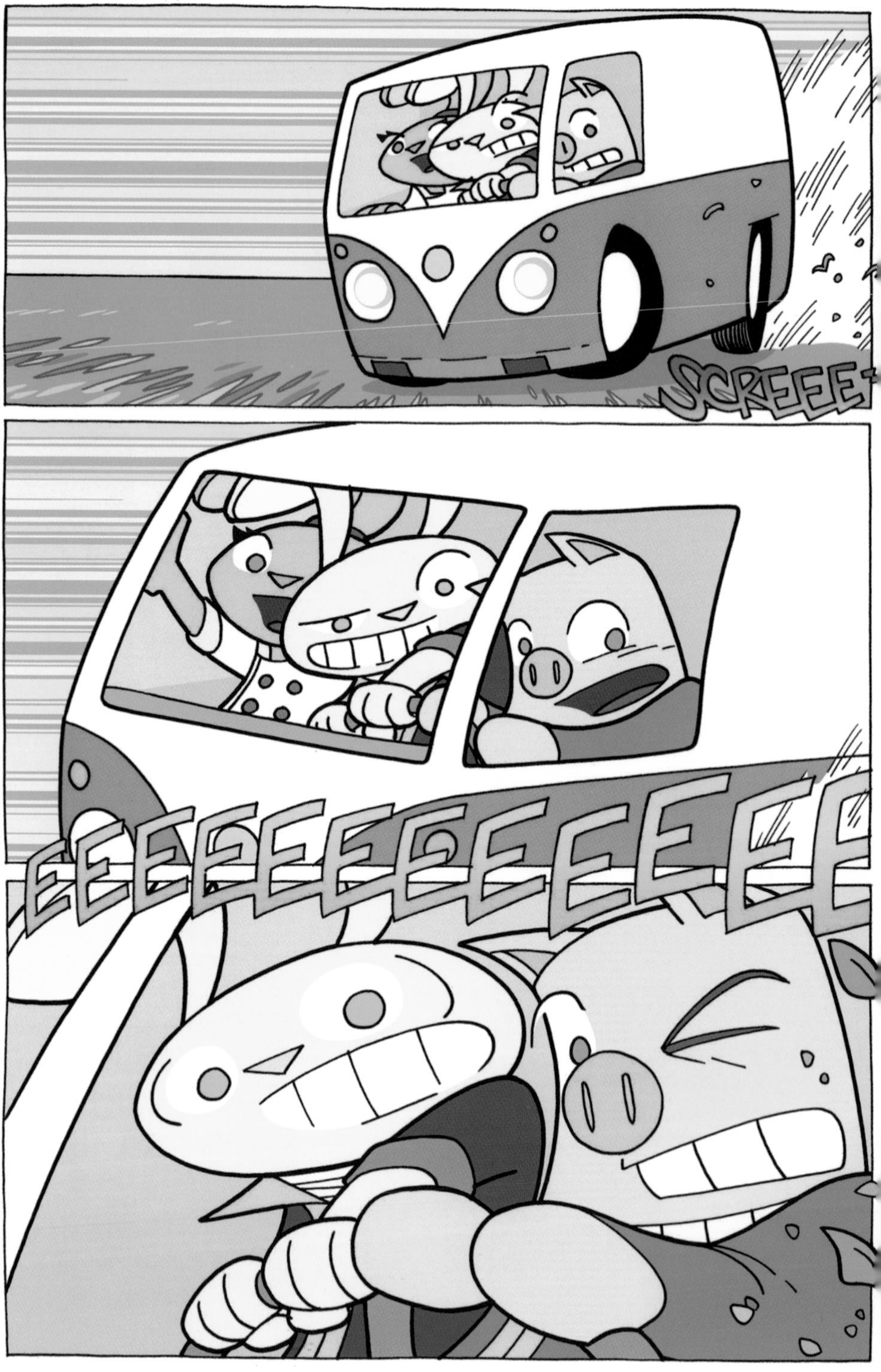
SCREEE-
EEEEEEEEEEEEEE-

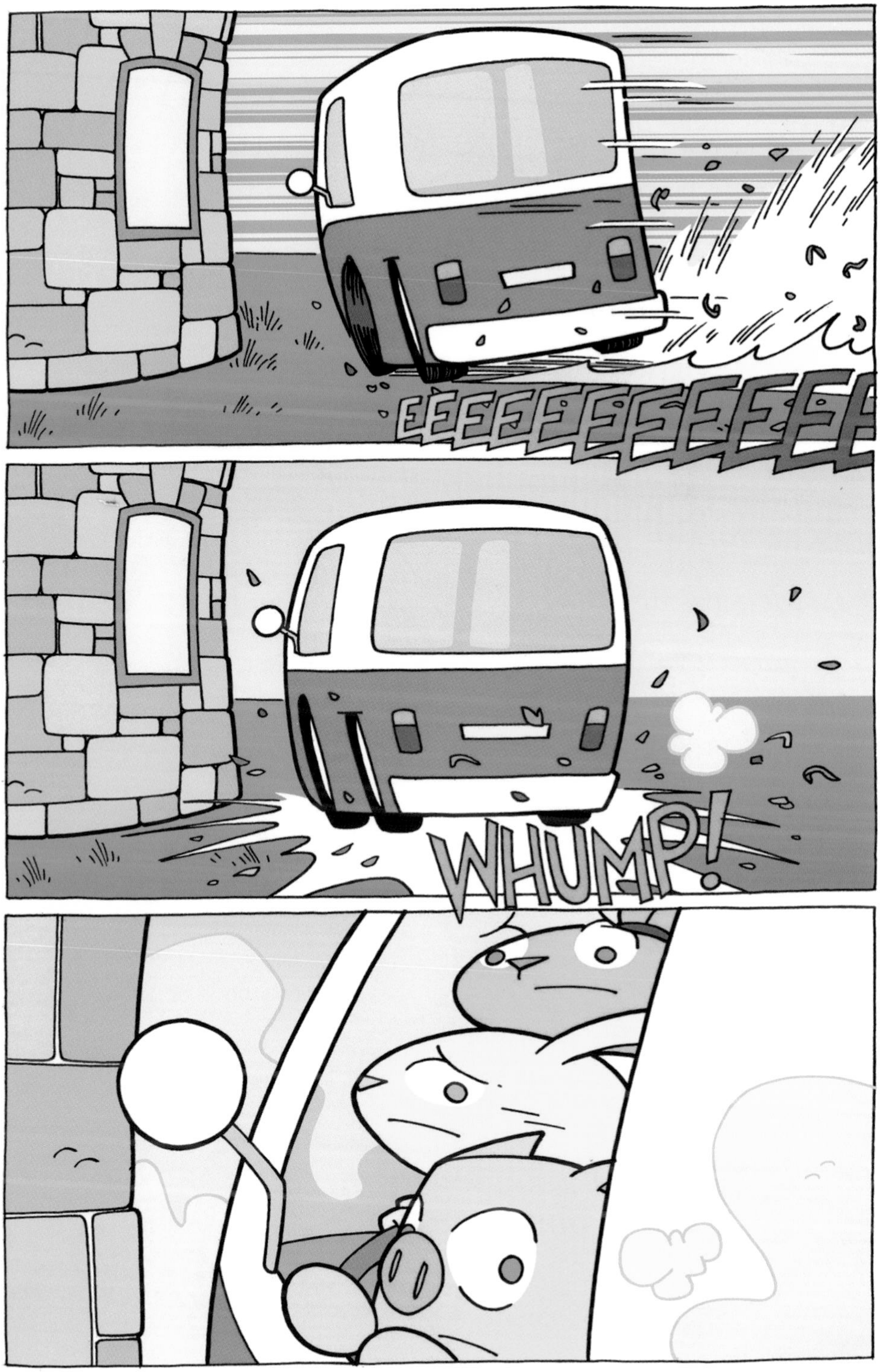
EEEEEEEEEEEEE
WHUMP!

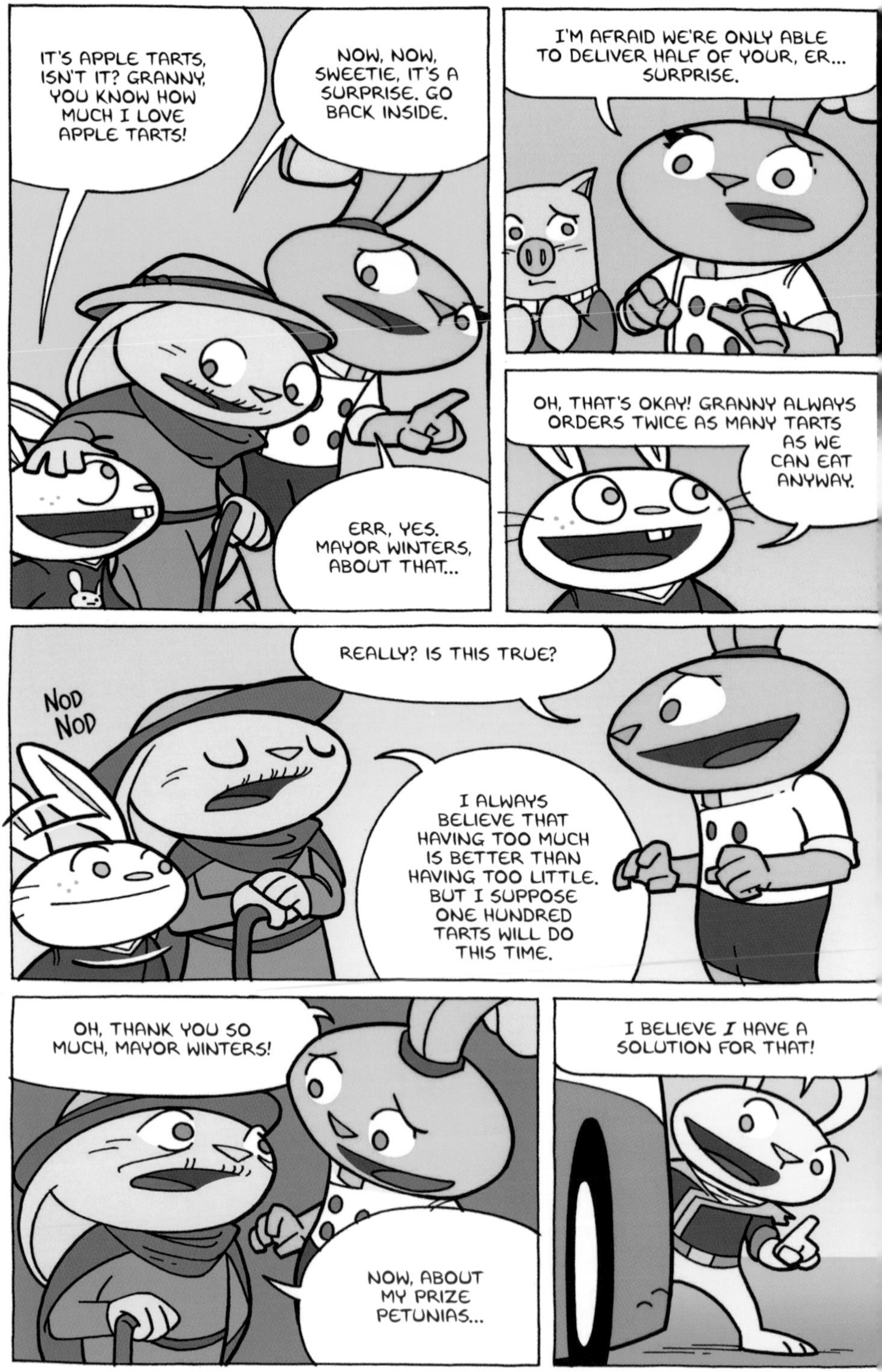
IT'S APPLE TARTS, ISN'T IT? GRANNY, YOU KNOW HOW MUCH I LOVE APPLE TARTS!
NOW, NOW, SWEETIE, IT'S A SURPRISE. GO BACK INSIDE.
ERR, YES. MAYOR WINTERS, ABOUT THAT...
I'M AFRAID WE'RE ONLY ABLE TO DELIVER HALF OF YOUR, ER... SURPRISE.
OH, THAT'S OKAY! GRANNY ALWAYS ORDERS TWICE AS MANY TARTS AS WE CAN EAT ANYWAY.
REALLY? IS THIS TRUE?
NOD NOD
I ALWAYS BELIEVE THAT HAVING TOO MUCH IS BETTER THAN HAVING TOO LITTLE. BUT I SUPPOSE ONE HUNDRED TARTS WILL DO THIS TIME.
OH, THANK YOU SO MUCH, MAYOR WINTERS!
NOW, ABOUT MY PRIZE PETUNIAS...
I BELIEVE *I* HAVE A SOLUTION FOR THAT!

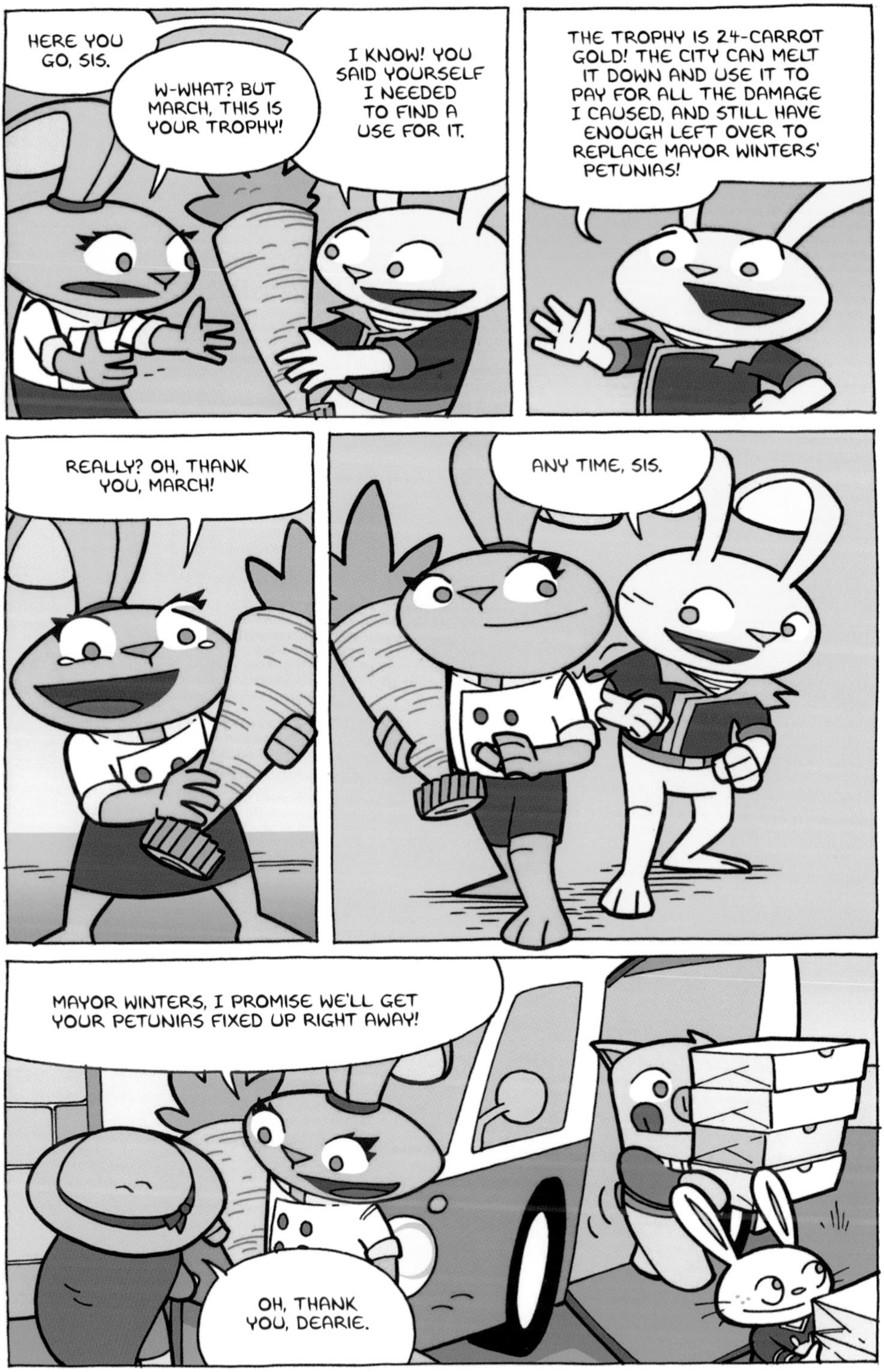
HERE YOU GO, SIS.
W-WHAT? BUT MARCH, THIS IS YOUR TROPHY!
I KNOW! YOU SAID YOURSELF I NEEDED TO FIND A USE FOR IT.
THE TROPHY IS 24-CARROT GOLD! THE CITY CAN MELT IT DOWN AND USE IT TO PAY FOR ALL THE DAMAGE I CAUSED, AND STILL HAVE ENOUGH LEFT OVER TO REPLACE MAYOR WINTERS' PETUNIAS!
REALLY? OH, THANK YOU, MARCH!
ANY TIME, SIS.
MAYOR WINTERS, I PROMISE WE'LL GET YOUR PETUNIAS FIXED UP RIGHT AWAY!
OH, THANK YOU, DEARIE.

44

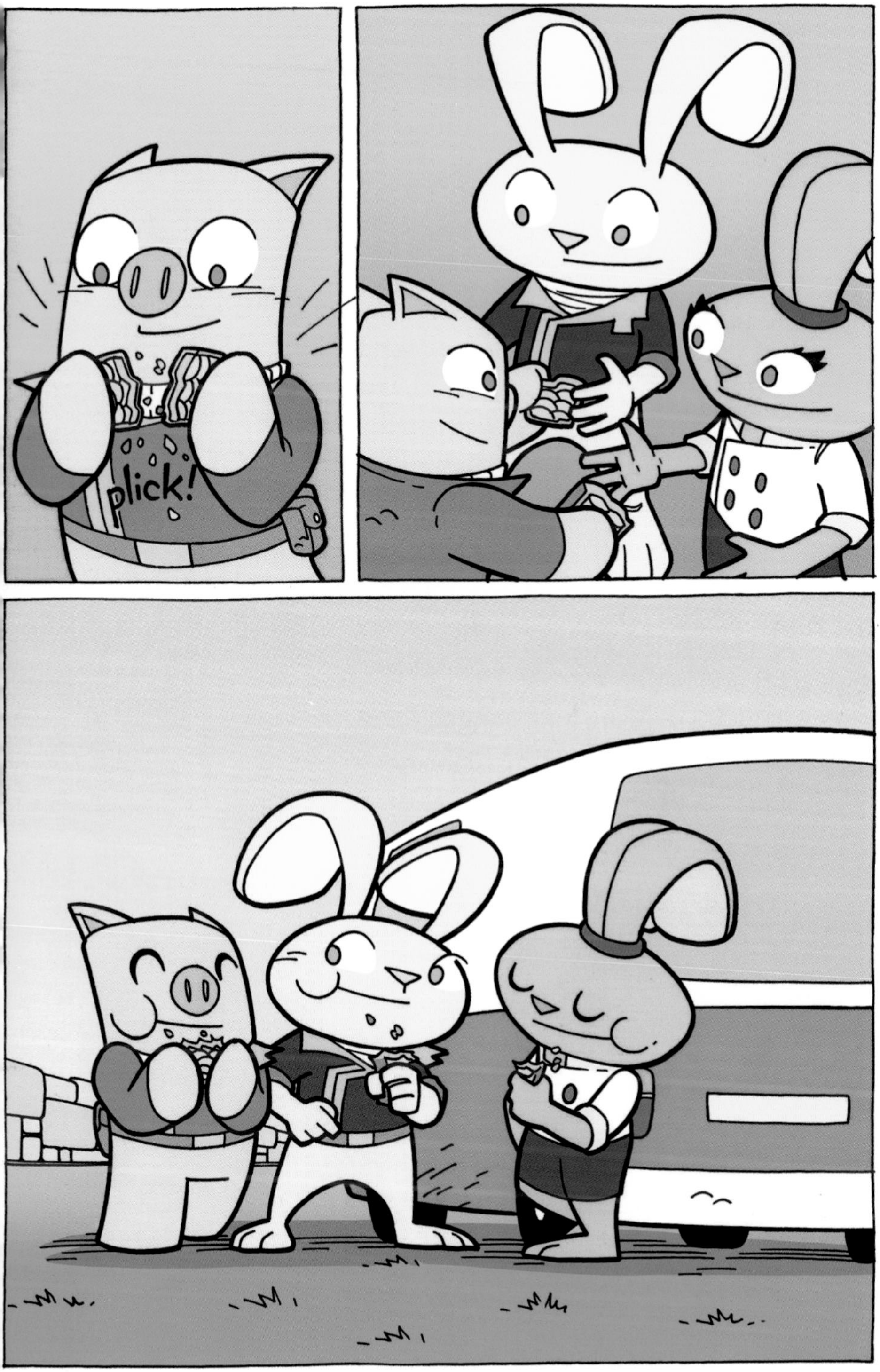
plick!

SKETCHES

1. Cover thumbnail rough

2. Inks

3. Colors & final corrections

4. Final cover

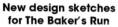

**New design sketches
for The Baker's Run**

MAROON
HAT
BAND

GRANNY
WINZERS

MAROON
CLOAK

LAVENDER
DRESS

APRIL'S DELIVERY
VAN
(NO REAR WINDOWS)

APRIL'S
SPRING
BAKERY

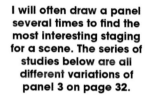

**I will often draw a panel
several times to find the
most interesting staging
for a scene. The series of
studies below are all
different variations of
panel 3 on page 32.**

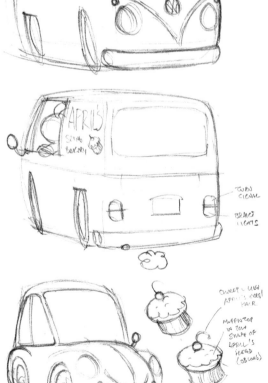

APRIL'S
SPRING
BAKERY

TURN
SIGNAL

BRAKE
LIGHTS

CURLY = UNE
APRIL'S CURLY
HAIR

MUFFIN TOP
IN TOP
SHAPE OF
APRIL'S
HEAD
(OBLONG)

KEAN SOO

Kean Soo was born in the United Kingdom, grew up in various parts of Canada and Hong Kong, trained as an electrical engineer, and now draws comics for a living. A former assistant editor and contributor for the FLIGHT comics anthology, Kean also created the award-winning Jellaby series of graphic novels.

Kean currently lives in Toronto with his wife, their dog Reginald Barkley, and their 1992 Volvo 940 Turbo.

Kean would also like to thank Judy Hansen, Donnie Lemke, Brann Garvey, Tony Cliff, Kazu Kibuishi, everyone in the FLIGHT crew, and Tory Woollcott for making March Grand Prix such a joy to work on.